When Fuzzy Was Afraid of Losing His Mother

For our families, with love — I.M. and J.C.

Published by
M A G I N A T I O N   P R E S S
An Educational Publishing Foundation Book
American Psychological Association
750 First Street, NE
Washington, DC 20002

For more information about our books, including a complete catalog, please write to us,
call 1-800-374-2721, or visit our website at www.maginationpress.com.

Editor: Darcie Conner Johnston
Designer: Susan K. White
Printed by Phoenix Color, Rockaway, New Jersey

Library of Congress Cataloging-in-Publication Data

Maier, Inger M.
When Fuzzy was afraid of losing his mother / written by Inger M. Maier ;
illustrated by Jennifer Candon.
p.   cm.
Summary: Fuzzy the sheep does not want his mother to leave his side,
but she finds a way to help him feel more secure about her absence.
ISBN 1-59147-168-0 (hardcover : alk. paper) — ISBN 1-59147-169-9 (pbk. : alk. paper)
[1. Separation anxiety—Fiction. 2. Mother and child—Fiction. 3. Sheep—Fiction.]
I. Candon, Jennifer, ill. II. Title.
PZ7.M27757Fu 2004
[E]—dc22   2004003588

Manufactured in the United States of America
10 9 8 7 6 5 4 3 2 1

When Fuzzy Was Afraid of Losing His Mother

written by Inger Maier, Ph.D.

illustrated by Jennifer Candon

MAGINATION PRESS • WASHINGTON, DC

Fuzzy the little sheep liked to run, skip, and jump with his little sheep friends. Sometimes they raced around the big rock in the middle of the field where they lived. Sometimes they jumped over puddles. And sometimes they looked for dandelion flowers to chew.

Fuzzy's mother liked to spend time with the other grown-up sheep by the big apple tree in the far corner of the field. There, they would happily chew on apples and la-a-a-augh and ba-a-a-ah about the news on the farm.

One day while Fuzzy was racing with his friends, he fell and skinned his little sheep knees. Big tears rolled down his face, and he ran to look for his mother. "Ma-a-ah!"

He looked and looked, but he couldn't find her. "I'm scared! Where are you?" he cried.

A few minutes later, Fuzzy's mother walked across the field with a big apple in her mouth. The little sheep ran to her and rubbed his face against her warm coat. "I thought you'd never come back," he baaah-ed. His little heart beat hard and fast until he calmed down.

After that, Fuzzy wouldn't let his mother out of his sight. He followed her everywhere. He stayed so close that if she stepped backwards or sideways, they would fall together in a woolly heap.

One day Fuzzy's mother said, "Tomorrow you can stay with Cousin Curley while I get apples."

"I can't, I can't," baaah-ed Fuzzy. "I'll miss you too much. And what if something happens to you?"

Fuzzy's mother nuzzled her little sheep. "Haven't I always come back? I'll bet if we counted, we would find out that I've come back more than 100 times."

Fuzzy thought about that and nodded his head. Yes, she always came back.

"So isn't it likely that I will come back tomorrow?"

Fuzzy nodded again. "Yes, likely… likely… likely."

The word 'likely' made him feel a little bit better.

Fuzzy's mother had more ideas. "Let's make a long dandelion chain to keep us tied together when I go to the apple tree."

"Okay," answered the little sheep. "Then I won't feel so lonely."

They made a long chain and walked through the farm until two lambs ate some of the flowers and broke the chain.

"What if I paint a big red circle on my back so you can see me from far away?"

"That's a good idea," smiled Fuzzy.

But some of the other sheep thought the red circle was such fun that they painted circles on each other, and Fuzzy couldn't recognize his mother.

"What if I ba-a-a-ah so loudly that you can hear me across the field?"

Fuzzy clapped as his mother stood up on her back legs, puffed out her chest, and let out a noise that was more like a ROAR-baaah than a baaah-baaah.

But the other sheep ran away in fright and told her that she could never, never do that again.

Fuzzy kept
following
his mother
everywhere
she went.

He still felt sad
and scared
when she was
out of sight.

Then she had a great idea.

"I know another way to help you," she smiled.
"You can use your imagination to think of pictures
and words that make you feel better."

Fuzzy looked
confused.

"Close your eyes,"
she explained.
"Now try to see a
picture of a flower
in your head."

"I see one," baaah–ed Fuzzy.

"Now think of me with a big
red circle on my back."

"I see!" Fuzzy giggled.

"You can also chase away
the pictures that make
you feel sad and scared,"
Fuzzy's mother said.
"Instead of thinking about
sad things, you can
imagine the apple tree.
Or a dandelion chain.
Or even my loud
ROAR–baaah."

"Or I can picture myself
chasing a butterfly,"
Fuzzy said. "Or an apple
falling next to my friend
Sleepy Hedgehog!"
He laughed.

"Remember this," Fuzzy's mother whispered. "You also have a very special blanket around you. It's invisible, but it has been there since you were born, and it's made with my love. So when you feel scared, you can imagine holding onto that blanket to help you feel warm and happy on the inside."

Fuzzy practiced imagining happy pictures in his head.

And he repeated the words, "likely, likely, likely."

After doing these things for a few days, he could let his mother walk a little farther away, and then farther still, without following her. At last, she could again join the other sheep by the apple tree.

At first it was hard, but
soon Fuzzy noticed that
he was much less scared.
Sometimes he only missed
his mother a teeny tiny
bit. She always came
back like she said she
would, and sometimes
she brought back
delicious apples and
dandelions.

One afternoon while they munched on apples, Fuzzy told his mother about racing his friends around the rock that morning, and jumping in the puddles with Cousin Curley.

His white woolly coat was brown with mud, and on his face was a big sheep smile.

"And guess what?"

"What?" Fuzzy's mother nuzzled her little sheep.

"I didn't feel scared even though you were away. I just felt haaaaaappy!"

Note to Parents

by Inger Maier, Ph.D.

Children can be expected to experience situations causing some anxiety, fear, or worry during the natural course of their development. However, some young children have excessive anxiety about separation from their home or a parent. They experience intense distress in anticipation of, for example, going to daycare or school, or visiting a friend. They may even be anxious about being in a different room from the parent during the day or at bedtime. Their anxious thoughts are associated with unpleasant sensations—such as stomachaches, nausea, headaches, and rapid heartbeat—which in itself can be frightening for the child.

Children's anxiety is related to their understanding of and thoughts about a situation, as well as their sense of competence to deal with it. Sometimes it appears to coincide with a specific event, such as an accident. Or the fear of separation may be a deflection of general distress relating to school, peer conflict, family stress, moving, loss of a pet, or any other significant event that makes the child feel an urgent need for reassurance and support.

Worry thoughts—"What if I get lost?" "What if you have an accident?"—increase the child's distress. The thoughts and images in the mind become the child's focus. At their young age, it's hard for them to filter out fears that are improbable.

Parents may understandably become upset, fatigued, and frustrated while attempting to understand, reason, and negotiate with the clinging child. Unfortunately, expressing anger or attempting to set strict limits only raises the child's distress. Also, a reward system featuring sticker charts and prizes for compliance may work for mild levels of anxiety but is often not helpful when the child is in a state of panic.

An alternative approach emphasizes correcting the worry thoughts and images that cause the anxiety. With this approach, parents help their children practice "realistic thoughts" that decrease rather than increase anxiety. Calming imagery, relaxation exercises such as deep breathing, and self-comforting activities such as drawing or hugging a blanket are also helpful. And finally, the child is encouraged to gather evidence against the worry thoughts.

The ideas and strategies suggested in this book and others in the **FUZZY THE LITTLE SHEEP** series are based on a cognitive-behavioral approach, which is frequently used in the treatment of anxiety. The basic principles are that thoughts, feelings, and behaviors are causally interrelated, and that new learning experiences with positive outcomes can be designed to change these thoughts, feelings, and behaviors in a healthy manner. *When Fuzzy Was Afraid of Losing His Mother* is based on the following ideas and guidelines for parents:

- Listen to your child's thoughts with respect. Help him label his feelings and describe physical sensations. Give reassurances: "I'm sorry you feel so upset. We can find ways to make you feel better."
- Rule out potential medical problems with the pediatrician, and think about what could be happening at home or school. Attempt to reduce stressors at home, and work with the school or daycare as needed. Talk with your child about any identified causes for the anxiety in simple terms.
- Correct your child's misconceptions by giving evidence. If she asks, "What if you don't come home?" you can respond with "I have come home [multiply her age by 365] days. So, is it likely I'll come home today?"
- Play the "likely or unlikely" game, taking turns asking silly questions. Focus on fantasy versus probability. For example: "Is it likely that an elephant will come into the kitchen?" "Is it likely you will brush your teeth today?"
- Because anxious children may hyperventilate or hold their breath, it's important to practice relaxed breathing. Say: "Keep your eyes open. Now breathe in s-l-o-w-l-y and catch your breath in your tummy. Slowly breathe out again and feel your tummy muscles move." Breathe with your child to demonstrate.
- Encourage your child to practice saying short "scripts" that are comforting to her, such as, "I only cried a little. I will be OK" or "Mom is thinking about me" or "My teacher looks after me."

- Use humor to help your child relax, but avoid ridicule or sarcasm.
- Practice imagining simple, pleasing images, such as a puppy, balloon, flower, or stuffed toy. Try the images Fuzzy's mother uses in this book, especially the "blanket of love." Think of these as calming photographs that can take the place of the scary photographs in the child's mind.
- Provide objects that your child finds comforting, such as stuffed animals, a blanket, or something belonging to you. Provide comforting activities as well, such as playing with a pet, reading books, listening to story tapes, or working on a craft project.
- Notice healthy changes in your child and talk about them. "Did you notice that you managed?" or "Did you notice that your tummy is much calmer?" or "I noticed that you had fun playing with your friend today" or "I noticed that you cried less when I needed to go out today. Didn't that feel better?" These are questions that make the child aware of positive outcomes, which will help alter thoughts about the situation.
- Remember that progress seldom happens immediately, and that small setbacks are likely. There will be times when you and your child feel frustrated and will need space and some time off.
- Create step-by-step challenges designed for success: for example, playing independently in different rooms in the home for gradually longer but realistic periods, or gradually introducing play-dates and activities outside of the home with increasing time and distance. Reassure your child about safe places and caregivers.
- Expand activities suited to her developmental stage, giving her an increased sense of competence and confidence.
- Occasionally review different coping tools with your child: comforting "self-talk" scripts, tummy breathing, imagery, evidence collecting, comforting articles, and so forth. Talk with him about ways he is managing to cope with anxiety and short periods of separation, and how much you are enjoying hearing about your child's day.